THE
PERFECT HORSE

The Double Diamond Dude Ranch

#4

Don't miss other exciting Chris adventures!

THE
PERFECT HORSE

The Double Diamond Dude Ranch
#4

By Louise Ladd

A TOM DOHERTY ASSOCIATES BOOK
NEW YORK

This is a work of fiction. All the characters and events portrayed in this book are either products of the author's imagination or are used fictitiously.

THE DOUBLE DIAMOND DUDE RANCH #4: THE PERFECT HORSE

Copyright © 1998 by Louise Ladd

First published in 1998 by Aerie Books Ltd.

A Tor Book
Published by Tom Doherty Associates, LLC
175 Fifth Avenue
New York, NY 10010

www.tor.com

Tor® is a registered trademark of Tom Doherty Associates, LLC.

ISBN: 0-812-55355-1

First Tor edition: July 2003

Printed in the United States of America

0 9 8 7 6 5 4 3 2 1

With Love to Erika Louise McKeon and her first
pony, Amber.

Acknowledgments

My deepest thanks to Jim and Bobbi Futterer, Executive Directors of the Dude Ranchers' Association. They have willingly answered my many questions, come up with a number of wonderful ideas, and generously shared their knowledge of, and love for, dude ranching.

And a warm thank you also to Ellen Hargrave and Tony Bronson at the Hargrave Ranch in Montana, and the Foster family at Lost Valley Ranch in Colorado.

chapter one

"Serena, I think it's time to start shopping for the perfect horse for you," I said as she brought Eagle to a halt in front of me.

It seemed like such a natural idea at the time. I wonder if I would have suggested it if I'd known the trouble it would lead to.

"Wow, Chris, do you really think I'm ready?" Serena's dark almond-shaped eyes sparkled like Christmas lights.

"Yup." I leaned on the pasture fence, my mare, Belle, standing quiet beside me. "You're handling Eagle real well now, and much sooner than I expected. He's a lot of horse, but you've got him going over those jumps like a jackrabbit."

"They're only small jumps," she said, trying to

sound modest. In truth, I knew she was pretty pleased with herself and she had a right to be.

I mounted Belle. "Why don't we ask your dad and mine to watch you ride, see if they agree."

"Oh gosh," Serena said. "If they say yes, I'll feel like I'm graduating from school!"

"Ugh, don't mention that word." I rode over and opened the pasture gate for her. "I can't believe school starts so soon. How did summer whiz by so fast?"

"It's been the best summer of my life," she said, riding through the gate. "I was crazy to think I didn't want to leave San Francisco."

The Changs had moved to Colorado last May, when they bought a ranch called the Lazy B partway down the mountain from us. Serena had arrived scared to death of horses and, with a little help from me, had finally turned into a rider good enough to be thinking of buying her own.

I was real proud of her. Even though we were the same age, going into sixth grade, I'd been her teacher. When you've lived on a dude ranch your whole life, riding comes as easy as walking, maybe easier.

We shut the gate and started back at a slow jog. I kept thinking how nice it was to have a best friend like Serena, another girl to share things with. Especially now that my old pal, Drew Diamond, who grew up with me on the ranch, was starting seventh grade and wanting to hang out with the guys more often. Not that we weren't still real good friends, but it wasn't like in the old days when it was just the two of us, always together.

"Can you and your father come over after supper?" I asked. "Dad will have time to watch you ride this evening. Most of the guests are on the overnight pack trip and the Double Diamond will be pretty quiet."

"Why didn't you go along on the trail?" Serena asked. "You usually do. Isn't it part of your job as a junior wrangler?"

"Drew's mom decided this is Get Ready for School night." I couldn't help making a face, just thinking about it.

Since my own mom left the ranch when I was six, Anna Diamond was one of the people who did mother-type things for me, along with Red Wing, our cook, and Maggie, our head wrangler. It was a good system. Instead of one, I had three different people I could go to with a problem, depending on the need. Anna was super at planning stuff.

Anna and her husband, Andy, owned the dude ranch. We had as many as two dozen guests staying with us during most of the year, to enjoy our mountain life and horseback riding. We also raised several hundred head of beef cattle. Andy mainly looked after the cows, while Anna loved to organize all the guests' social events, like cookouts, sing-alongs, hayrides and parties.

"What is Get Ready for School night?" Serena asked.

"Anna drags Drew and me into our bedrooms and

3

goes over our clothes, checking to see what new stuff we need to buy."

"It sounds like you'll be busy then. Maybe I should ask Dad to come over another time."

"No! I'll do anything to get out of it! How can you think of wool sweaters and snow boots in August when it's still so hot?"

"It's weird to be starting school so early," she said. "In California we didn't have to go back until after Labor Day."

"I know, I hate it too. But remember how it was last year, when we got out in early June? The mountains were all fresh and green, and the pastures were full of foals and calves. June's one of the prettiest months in the Rockies and it's great to be free to enjoy it."

We reached a meadow and urged the horses into a good fast run. My mare, Belle, was expecting a foal come winter and I liked to keep her well exercised so she'd be in peak condition. We raced through the meadow and up a rise, then down through an aspen grove, only slowing when we neared the ranch.

Back at the corral, while we unsaddled Serena said, "I can't believe you think I'm ready to look for my own horse! And I know just what I want—a palomino!"

"A horse's good nature is more important than the color of its coat," I said.

"Then I'll get a palomino with a good nature!"

I laughed. "Let's wait and see what Dad says.

He's the horse expert." My dad was ranch foreman, and also in charge of breeding the dozen or so colts and fillies we raised each year. What he didn't know about horses would fit in a baby's bootie.

"Gee, I hope he thinks I'm ready," Serena said. "I sure *feel* ready. And excited! But are you sure tonight's the best time for us to come over?"

"Why not? It stays light out until almost nine."

"I mean about Anna and your school clothes."

"It's perfect," I said. "This way, I can tell Anna to order whatever she wants and I'll wear it."

"You're kidding!" Serena stared at me. "Don't you like to choose your own clothes?"

I shrugged. "Jeans, shirts, sweaters—they're all pretty much the same. What difference does it make?"

"But what about the new styles and all?" Serena asked.

"Anna knows more about that than I do. Don't worry, I'll make out just fine."

Serena shook her head, grinning. "I guess you will. You always do."

Just as I suspected, Anna was a bit relieved to find out she wouldn't have to argue with me about clothes. I always wanted the plainest jeans and shirts, and she liked me to dress the way the other girls did. I knew she'd pull out a pile of magazines and study up on the newest fashions, then go down the mountain to scout out what the town girls thought was "hot." As long as she didn't overdo it, I figured I could live with her choices.

Besides, now that I was going into sixth grade, maybe it was time I began to dress more like the other girls. I'd made a stab at trying to copy them this summer, but it was like trying to nail a pony's horseshoe onto a race horse—not a real good fit.

Still, with Serena's mom giving my boring-brown hair a decent cut now and then, and Anna in charge of my clothes, maybe I could fool people into thinking I cared about something other than horses, which I didn't.

Right after supper, Serena's whole family drove up in their jeep. Besides Mr. and Mrs. Chang, there were three brothers, Tommy, Matt and David, all in high school or college. I guess they were curious to see how well their little baby sister could ride, now that she had pushed past her fear of horses.

"I *begged* them not to come," Serena said as she followed me into the corral where I had Eagle saddled and waiting. "I feel like I'm taking final exams in front of the whole world!"

"Easy now," I said. "There's no reason to be nervous. You'll do fine. Just remember you're in charge, not Eagle, and put him over the rails the way you've been doing."

"You hear that, Eagle?" she asked, taking him gently by the jaws and looking into his eyes. "You make a fool of me and I won't let you jump at all tomorrow."

It was a dire threat. Eagle loved jumping, unlike

most cow ponies. He was always delighted to find a rider who shared his opinion.

We'd set up several low jumps in the pasture down by the pond and I followed Serena through the gate, riding Belle.

Besides the Changs, several of the guests had collected along the fence, including Mr. Harris. He'd been a top rodeo winner in his day but was too creaky with age to ride anymore. Still, he loved the ranch life so he came to us every summer to get away from "that blasted retirement home and those old folks," as he put it. He was a popular guest, always willing to share a few tales of the old days.

Until this summer. Somehow the spirit had gone out of Mr. Harris and no one knew why. He'd play a game of bridge, or sing along with the others when Jamie pulled out his guitar, but he spent a lot of time on the porch staring out at the Rocky Mountain peaks that surrounded our valley. Whatever was troubling him, he wouldn't say. Still, he was one of my favorite guests.

"Gosh, do they all have to watch?" Serena asked me, staring at the small group lining the fence.

"Pretend they're not there," I said. "Or think of them as scarecrows, stuffed with straw. It's just you and Eagle who count, so keep your mind on your horse and you'll do fine."

She flashed me a nervous smile, then I saw her settle herself and Eagle into the partnership she was so good at forming, no matter which horse she rode.

She gave the credit to a trick I'd taught her when she first started to ride. "Exchanging breaths helps a lot," she'd say whenever I commented on how well she was doing.

It's an odd but interesting fact that if you greet a horse the same way they greet each other, it speeds up the friendship process. When horses meet, they huff into each others' noses, sort of the way we shake hands. Serena first tried exchanging breaths with a colt, and since then had made it a habit as she moved up in her riding skills, advancing from Sneakers to Bumper to Eagle.

"Have fun," I called as she rode off. I crossed my fingers for her, hoping I'd taught her well enough to pass the test.

She loped down to the far end of the pasture, then turned Eagle toward the first of the six low jumps. He skimmed over it, and took the next three with the same ease. At the fifth, he was going a little fast but slowed the moment Serena gave him the signal. He sailed over it, and the last one, as smooth as butter.

Serena grinned, then urged Eagle into a fast run, racing along the pasture fence for the pure joy of it. Finally, she brought him to a neat halt in front of her dad and mine.

Belle and I rode over to hear their comments.

"Well, Lew, what do you say?" Dad asked Mr. Chang. Serena had told me his name in Chinese was actually "Lu," but he long ago began spelling it the American way to avoid confusion.

"Well now, Bart," Mr. Chang said slowly, drawing it out to tease Serena, "I'd have to say my little girl can ride some. But as to getting her a horse of her own . . ."

Mai Chang poked her husband in the ribs. "Cut it out, you two. Don't keep her in suspense. Serena, you were great! You've learned so much in such a short time. If I could reach you up on that horse, I'd give you a hug!"

"I guess your wife has made up your mind for you, Lew," Dad said, winking.

"As usual," Mr. Chang said. "So, Serena, it looks like we'll be going horse-shopping soon."

"Alll riiight!" She tore off her hat and threw it in the air. "Can we start tomorrow?"

Everyone laughed, pleased with her eagerness.

"I could make a few calls tomorrow," Dad said. "But it's a little early in the fall for most of the local ranchers to be selling off stock. I did hear there'd be an auction though, not too far from here, a week from Saturday. A bunch of horses brought down from the north, where the winter weather comes early."

"An auction!" Serena said. "That would be so much fun."

"Well, we'll go take a look," Mr. Chang said. "But don't expect to come home with anything. We have to find the right horse for you, and that might take some time."

"Sure, we'll just take a look," Serena agreed,

10

but I wondered if she meant it. She was so excited I wasn't sure we could rein her in when the time came.

Another kind of excitement—*not* the good kind—was waiting for me that night when I finally got back to the cabin I shared with Dad.

Usually we pick up our mail in the main lodge, but someone had slipped a letter addressed to me under the door. I'd been so busy that day I hadn't gone near the office, so Anna, or maybe Red Wing, thought they'd be helpful.

If they wanted to be *really* helpful, they should have burned the darn thing.

The letter was from the school principal. I tore open the envelope, not stopping to wonder what the news might be.

"Oh no!" I ran for the phone and dialed Serena's number. When she answered I said, "Did you get a letter from the school today?"

"Yes," Serena said. "Why are you so upset? It only says that instead of having Mr. Cox, like they told us we would, we have a different teacher because they had to rearrange the classes."

"Did you get assigned to the same teacher I did?" I asked, my heart full of dread. "Did you get Mrs. Brown?"

"Yes, did you? Gosh, I hope we're in the same class."

"We are," I said in a funeral voice. "At least we'll be wading through the same mud hole together."

"What's wrong with Mrs. Brown?" she asked in panic.

"She's only the strictest teacher in the whole United States," I said. "They call her "Homework" Brown, and for a good reason. Get ready—it's going to be a *very long* year."

chapter two

"Hurry up, Chris, or you'll miss the school bus!" Anna called from the station wagon parked outside the kitchen door.

"Coming!" I jammed a couple more pencils in my backpack, wondering what I was forgetting. "Where's Drew?"

"I'm in the car!" he shouted. "Let's go!"

That was new. In past years, we had to drag Drew out the door each morning. But now that he was starting seventh grade, I'd already seen changes in him, and suspected I'd be seeing a few more. Not a happy thought.

In the past, Drew and I always agreed that the first day of school is the worst day of the year. It's so hard to leave the ranch, which is full of families on vacation. Lots of kids don't have to be home until after Labor Day, so it feels like our summer is suddenly cut short while everyone else is still enjoying theirs.

Honk! Honk!

"I'm coming!" I glanced around the kitchen. Did I have everything?

"Don't forget your lunch." Red Wing, our cook, handed me a sack.

"Thanks." I crammed it in the backpack, quickly kissed her wrinkled cheek, and ran out to the car.

As Anna turned down the drive, I twisted in the seat, trying to keep my eyes on the corral and barn as long as I could.

This morning, instead of walking out into the dewy pasture at first light to bring in the horses, I'd been getting dressed for school. Instead of joining in the jokes and laughter with the wranglers while we did the morning chores, Drew and I ate a hearty breakfast under Red Wing's careful eye, then let Anna fuss over us, making sure we had all our school supples and our hair and clothes were fixed just right.

In the mornings to come, we'd be hunting for overdue library books, or trying to finish up the last of our homework assignments, all the while worrying about missing the bus that picked us up at the foot of the mountain. Then there'd be the long ride into town with the rowdy boys and the giggling girls, and waiting at the end of it, a full day stuck inside the building.

Starting today, I was switching one life—the natural one—for another full of schedules and bells and closed-in walls and sitting still and only speaking when called on.

And now, this year, Mrs. Brown was added to all the other joys of school.

The only bright spot was that I had Serena to suffer alongside me. Partway down the mountain, Anna turned into the Lazy B and Serena came banging out the door, full of smiles. The auction was this coming Saturday and she could barely think of anything but getting her own horse.

Dad had called around, but hadn't found a suitable one for sale yet. He warned Serena it might take some time and she said yes-yes, she understood, but I thought she was secretly counting on finding her perfect horse at the auction.

"Hi, Drew!" she said, bouncing into the car. "Hey, Chris, you look great!"

"Thanks. You do too." I meant it. Her shiny black hair curved around her cheeks and she wore a cherry-red shirt over a matching short skirt.

"Thanks for picking me up, Mrs. Diamond," Serena said. "My mom says she'll meet the bus this afternoon, then help you figure out your computer problem when she drops off Chris and Drew at your ranch."

"That will be fine," Anna said. She and Mrs. Chang had become good friends while Serena's mom, who was a computer expert, taught Anna how to tame her new PC. They got along well, and I thought Anna was a happier person now that the Changs had moved so close to us.

"Gosh, Chris," Serena said. "I hardly recognized you, you're dressed so nice. Where did you get that cool shirt?"

"Anna bought it in town." It was much too stylish for my tastes, but I'd made a bargain with Anna and I had to wear it. At least I'd insisted on my old jeans—not the *real* old soft ones, but a broken-in comfortable pair.

Serena talked about horses all the way down to the bus stop. A dozen kids were waiting, and it was sort of like a reunion. We were ranchers' kids and most of us hadn't seen each other since June because we lived so far apart.

Drew immediately paired up with Jimmy Thorne, who was also in seventh grade. Jimmy wore thick glasses and looked like a nerd, but I'd seen him lassoing calves and riding broncos at the rodeo and he was no sissy, I can tell you.

The only two kids in my class, besides Serena, were the Hatcher twins. Zeke and Josh looked so much alike that if they stood facing each other you'd wonder where the mirror was.

They were both blond, brawny—and boring, in my opinion. They never spoke a word that didn't have to do with football, basketball or hockey.

"Quit staring." I nudged Serena, who was sneaking peeks at the Hatchers. "They look much better than they taste."

She rolled her eyes at me. "Very funny."

But I noticed she didn't say much after that. Now that we were surrounded by other kids, she'd gone back to being the shy, quiet girl almost no one noticed in class last spring.

I kept glancing at her during the bus ride into town. I figured it was up to me to see that she got to know people. I had lots of friends in school, although not a *best* friend, like Serena.

Everyone seemed to like me, and I liked them, but we just didn't have a whole lot to talk about. Somehow I just couldn't get too excited about which girl had a crush on which boy, and who said what to who, and what they said back. Dad told me maybe I'd grow into that kind of stuff, or maybe I wouldn't, but it didn't really matter because he liked me fine the way I was. That was a comforting thought.

When the bus pulled up in front of the school building, we all poured off. There were lots of shrieks and shouts as kids spotted their friends, and checked out who was wearing what and how different people had changed over the summer.

"Hi, Chris!" Jeanne waved at me from a cluster of girls over by the spruce tree. She was a good friend and I'd gone to her sleep-over party that summer, which turned out to be the least thrilling event of my life, though it was no fault of hers.

"Come on, Serena," I said. "I'll introduce you."

"That's okay," she said, hanging back. "You go ahead."

"No way." I took her by the arm. "Come on, they won't bite, I promise. Jeanne's real nice, and so are Cindy and Kirsten. You'll like them."

"I—I know, most of them were in our class when I moved here at the end of last semester. You don't have to introduce me. I already know them."

"But they don't know *you*. Now, you can't spend the whole year like a mouse in the corner, so you might as well get it over with."

Still she hung back. "I don't know what to say to them."

"You don't have to say much for starters," I said. "They all have plenty to talk about. Just join the group and nod in the right places. They'll think you're a genius if you're a good listener."

Serena sighed, but she let me lead her over to the girls under the tree.

"Hi, everyone," I said. "You all know Serena, don't you? She lives just down the mountain from me, on the Wright's old ranch, the Lazy B."

"Hi," several said, or "How are you doing, Serena?" Or, "Good to see you again."

Then they went back to talking about the summer. Cindy took a trip to New England, where they went out whale watching. Kirsten said they went to Atlantic City and her dad spent all his time in the casinos but *she* got a great tan and met a really cute lifeguard. Jeanne said she stayed home and made lots of money baby-sitting, Tammy said her summer was a total bore, Sandra said hers was too, except that a really hunky eighth-grader moved in next door and he spent a lot of time working out with weights right under her bedroom window so it wasn't a total waste.

Partway through all this, I winked at Serena. She grinned back, saying without words, "You were right."

I finally broke into Sandra's description of the hunk's chest muscles. "Did any of you get a letter about switching teachers?"

"Yes!" Jeanne said. "I can't believe it! Did you get stuck with Mrs. Brown too?"

"Serena and I both did," I said. "Isn't it awful? We were supposed to have Mr. Cox and he's so cool. Why did *we* have to be switched to "Homework" Brown?"

Cindy laughed. "Poor you. I'm glad it's not me."

"I got her too." Tammy swung her long blond hair, a move that my pal Drew and his friends found fantastic, to judge by their comments. "It's a real drag."

The bell rang and the mob of kids rushed for the door like stampeding cattle. I couldn't see why they were so eager to be penned up. Serena and I followed slowly, and made our way down the crowded halls to our new room.

Mrs. Brown stood behind her desk, smiling as she watched us file in. She was an ordinary, middle-aged person, not pretty, not ugly, not tall, not short, not anything in particular except *strict*. She'd been teaching forever so her reputation was well known.

"Welcome, class. Will everyone please take a seat." Those were plain, everyday words, but it was the way she spoke them. Everyone hopped to, scrambling to find a desk in the back of the room.

Serena and I weren't quick enough. We ended up stuck in the first row, of all bad luck.

The moment the final bell rang, "Homework" Brown whipped out the attendance list and put on the glasses that dangled from a chain around her neck. "When I call your name, please answer, 'present.'"

The first three kids did as she asked. Then one of the boys, a show-off named Rich Darrow, said "Yo" when she read his name.

Mrs. Brown simply looked at him. And looked. And looked. The room was deadly quiet.

Finally, Rich Darrow's smirk faded. "Present," he said in a sullen voice.

Mrs. Brown didn't comment, just went on reading off the list. One or two people said "Here" by mistake, but switched over to "Present" real fast.

Attendance done, she took off her glasses and studied us, looking into our eyes one by one. It was like being pinned under a microscope.

"I look forward to getting to know each one of you," she said. "I believe we will have a very good, productive year together."

It sounded like a jail sentence.

"I'm sure you have a number of questions, and I'll be glad to answer them, but first let me explain how this class will function." Mrs. Brown stood behind her desk, back straight, chin up. "Let me begin by expressing my philosophy of education. It's quite simple. You are in school to learn."

She stopped speaking. The room was so quiet we could hear the sunshine hitting the windowpanes, I swear.

"That is my philosophy," she said after a moment. "Let me repeat it, to be sure you understand quite clearly. You are in school to learn."

Once again, silence.

"Good." She nodded. "Now you understand that all other activities are mere side benefits. And since you are here to learn, let me explain how that will come about. First, you learn by paying attention in class. You also learn by studying, both in school and at home. You will have homework assignments every night, and those assignments will be turned in on time. I do not accept excuses, or requests for extensions. Your assignments will be done, and they will be done on time."

She stopped speaking and her eyes went around the room again, face by face. "Is that quite clear? Let me repeat it once again. I do not accept excuses. There is no point in asking, no matter what the situation, because the answer is and will be: no."

Another silence, then she nodded and her face relaxed into a smile. Actually, a nice smile. "Good, now that we understand each other, let's move on to other subjects. First, long-term assignments. I will give you a novel to read and write a report on—a different book for each of you. These are enjoyable books, but they are also examples of good literature . . ."

The rest of the day went on like that. We did the usual start-of-school stuff like signing out textbooks and lockers, passing out notices and making a list of special supplies Mrs. Brown required us to keep handy, like at least six sharpened pencils and our own scissors, ruler and calculator.

None of it was different from regular school life, except the weird silence when Mrs. Brown was speaking. No whispers, no giggles, no note-passing. Early on, a few kids tried to get away with stuff and got hit with that ice-cold silent stare. After that no one dared try, not even Rich Darrow.

During assembly lunch, gym, and tours of the library and computer room, we were pretty normal, but even then we went around feeling slightly shocked, and were quieter than we might have been.

When the final bell rang at the end of the day, Mrs. Brown was in the middle of giving out the homework assignments. Instead of shoving things into our desks and packs, we waited until she finished, then left the classroom at a walk, not a run, no matter how eager we were to get out of there.

23

And wow, were we eager! We exploded down the halls like fizz from an over-shook soda bottle. Boys hooted and hollered, girls shrieked and squealed, complaints and smart remarks flew back and forth.

I'd never been so glad to step outside in my life. It felt like I'd just spent forty years in prison. Fresh air, sunshine, freedom—how I'd missed it!

"Bye, Chris! See you tomorrow, Serena," Jeanne called as she ran for her bus.

I was pleased. We'd had lunch with Jeanne and Cindy and Kirsten and, while no one made a fuss over Serena, they didn't ignore her either. It was a good first step.

Once we were on our bus, I said to Serena, "I can't believe it, but "Homework" Brown's even tougher than people said. Do you think she'll stay this way *all year*?"

"Probably." She was in the aisle seat and one of the Hatcher twins went past, headed for the back of the bus where the older boys always sat. He glanced down just as she glanced up. They both looked away quickly.

"How are we going to live through it?" I asked.

She shrugged. "It's not so bad if we just do the work like she wants. Anyway, I'm going to have my own palomino, and nothing else really matters. I can't wait till the auction on Saturday!"

"Serena, I told you before, you can't choose a horse just because of his color. There are a lot more important things to look for."

24

The Perfect Horse

"I know! You've told me, Dad's told me, your father's told me. Well, you can all pick out any horse you like, and any color you like—as long as he's gold with a blond mane!"

Uh oh, I thought, I just hope this trail we're headed down doesn't lead to big trouble.

chapter three

A surprise was waiting on the porch of the Double Diamond ranch house when Mrs. Chang drove us home from the bus that afternoon. It was a big package—huge—addressed to Dad and me.

"Wow, Anna, can I open it now?" I searched for a return address and saw it came from Westport, Connecticut. "Do I have to wait until Dad gets in at suppertime?"

"I don't think he'd mind if you went ahead," Anna said.

Mr. Harris, the retired rodeo rider, was in his rocker and looked over with a certain interest as Drew, Serena, Anna and Mrs. Chang watched me rip the carton open. On top of a thick pile of those curly styrofoam squigglies they use for packing was a letter, also addressed to Dad and me.

Dear Bart and Chris, it read. *I found this at an estate sale and thought of you both. Perhaps Chris would like to try it, but if not, you might have an occasional guest on the ranch who would like to use it. I know your horses are trained for Western riding, but I couldn't pass up such a great bargain. I have no need of it myself, so please feel free to use it any way you choose. With fondest regards, Amanda Morris.*

Mrs. Morris was one of our regular guests. She was a widow who'd stayed with us for a month this past summer and had only gone back East a short while ago. She and my Dad had become . . . well, good friends, and I liked her a lot, too. Even if it took me a while to discover the fact.

"Who is it from?" Serena asked.

I handed her the letter and told her to read it out loud while I began to dig through the squigglies, wondering what could be underneath them.

"Careful, Chris," Anna said. "I don't want that stuff scattered all over. Let me get something to catch them."

"Hurry, please," I said. "I can't wait to see what Mrs. Morris sent!"

Anna was back in a minute with a tablecloth we spread under the box. I began to scoop out the squigglies.

"It's leather . . ." I reported. "It's real fine leather . . . it's a saddle!"

I held it up, brushing off the plastic bits that still clung to it.

"It's an English saddle!" I ran my hand over it, enjoying the feel of the old, soft, carefully worked leather. "It's a real beauty, too."

"Sure is," Drew said. "But what are you going to do with it?"

I shook my head, wondering myself.

"It's so *small* compared to a regular saddle, isn't it?" Serena said.

Drew said, "It doesn't even have a saddlehorn."

"You're used to Western saddles," Anna said. "I grew up in the East and I recognize this. It's for riding dressage." She pronounced it, dress-*aage*.

"What's that?" Serena asked.

"Have you ever seen the Lipizzaner stallions perform on TV?" Anna said. "You know, those beautiful white stallions from the Spanish Riding School?"

"You mean the ones that leap through the air, and ride crisscross patterns?" Serena said. "Is that dressage?"

Anna nodded. "Few horses can leap like that, but some of the best ones can learn a lot of difficult moves that are woven into all sorts of patterns."

I was still stroking the soft leather saddle. "Do you think Belle could learn?"

"Maybe," Anna said. "Do you remember Mrs. Walsh, who stays with us every fall? She rides in competition back East and we were talking about it one night. She said a lot of the moves are similar to what a well-trained cow pony already knows—how to balance himself, and make quick turns, for instance. He uses many of the same muscles for dressage as he does for working cattle."

"No kidding!" I looked up to the pasture where Belle was grazing peacefully. There was no doubt my mare was an expert cutting horse. "Do you think Mrs. Walsh might teach Belle and me when she gets here?"

"She might," Anna said. "She's good enough to perform the *Kür*. That's when you make up your own routine, set to music. It's something like freestyle ice skating, but you're dancing on four hooves instead of two blades."

"Dancing on four hooves . . ." I repeated. A picture grew in my mind, Belle and me, dancing together to music . . . What could be more wonderful?

A sudden black cloud of fur exploded through the door and leaped into the pile of white squigglies, sending them flying. With the breeze blowing down from the mountains, it was like a blizzard had hit the porch.

"Star!" Drew tried to grab his puppy, now grown as big as a young bear cub. "Star, no! Cut that out!"

The pup jumped up and kissed his face, sending more styrofoam snow whirling into the air.

"Drew, get that dog out of here!" Anna ordered.

"I'm trying!" Drew reached for Star's collar but the puppy did a quick half-twist and threw himself back into the pile of squigglies, rolling in delight, his long furry tail going a mile a minute. Fake snow flew.

"No, Star!" "Come here, Star!" "Sit, boy!" "Grab him!" We tried to catch the big pup, but he was too fast. He whirled, he spun, he wagged that tail, then he took off, running toward the corral, trailing curly styrofoam bits all the way.

Drew followed at a gallop, shouting out commands Star wasn't about to obey.

Anna stood watching them, hands on her hips, totally fed up. The rest of us were laughing so hard our sides hurt. Even our guest, Mr. Harris, was chuckling, his faded blue eyes full of life again.

"What am I going to do with that monster?" Anna watched him disappear into the barn, then turned around and saw us holding our ribs, giggling and guffawing. She allowed herself a tiny smile while she shook her head in disgust. "Just look at this mess!"

"Monster!" I gasped out. "That's the perfect name for him! Let's call him Monster!"

"Monster!" Serena laughed. "All in favor say "Aye!"

"Aye!" "Aye!" "Aye!" we shouted.

Anna nodded. "Star's name is officially changed to Monster. Now how am I going to get this porch cleaned up?"

Naturally she knew that would get her the volunteers she needed. Anna is a smart lady.

We'd just dumped the last load of squigglies in the trash can when Maggie, our head wrangler, returned, leading the trail ride. I went over to help unsaddle, and Maggie asked me to work with a couple of the young buckaroos in the corral. They needed extra coaching and she knew I enjoyed teaching the little kids.

I didn't exactly *forget* about my homework, but figured I'd do it that night. Why waste a blue-sky afternoon in the cabin? Then, after supper, Anna got everyone to join in a game of charades and I hung around the lodge for a while, watching the fun.

By the time I got to the cabin Dad and I share, it was getting close to bedtime. When you're used to getting up at five in the morning, it's hard to keep your eyes open much later than nine.

I pulled out my schoolbooks and began the math assignment, but after a while the numbers began to spin in my head. I jotted down whatever answers I could, then plowed through English, trying to diagram a whole string of sentences.

The next thing I knew, Dad was guiding me to bed. I'd fallen asleep with my head in the book. Oh well, I figured I'd do the rest in the morning over breakfast.

That didn't quite work out, and "Homework" Brown was not real thrilled with my half-finished papers. I had to stay in at recess and complete them. Then they came back covered with so many X's, I had to redo it all over again during lunch. It sure made for a long day.

By the time I got home, I was determined to get

right to my books, but I'd forgotten Anna had planned a Sunset Ride, where we all take the trail over to the lake for a big cookout, followed by the talent show, with both guests and staff getting up in front of everyone, making fools of themselves for the most part. Now, how could I miss that?

Friday I spent recess and lunch doing—and redoing—homework again.

At last, *at last*, AT LAST it was Saturday.

The day of the horse auction.

"I didn't sleep one minute last night," Serena said when Dad and I reached the Lazy B in the early hours of Saturday morning. The sun was barely up and their lights were on, giving the yellow kitchen a cheerful glow. "All I could think about was finding my horse."

Her mother handed Mr. Chang a big thermos of coffee. "Now Serena, you've always been a sensible girl," she said, closing the top of a cooler packed with food. "Don't get carried away and expect to find the right one today."

"I know, I know." Serena wasn't truly listening. "I have his stall all ready. I even filled up the water bucket!"

Dad and her parents exchanged looks. Finally Dad shrugged and said, "Let's hope we get lucky then."

Mr. Chang drove, and Dad sat up front with him. Mrs. Chang, Serena and I climbed into the backseat. We towed the horse trailer behind us—just in case.

33

It was a long drive to the town where the auction was held, but we got there just as it was beginning. The first lot of horses up for sale were yearlings, and, of course, too young to ride.

"We should be looking for a gelding between seven and ten years old," Dad said. "We want one who's old enough to be well trained, but young enough to give you plenty of years of riding ahead, Serena. Let's go check out the stock."

"Why a gelding?" she asked. "Why not a mare like Chris has?"

"Mares can be difficult at times," Dad explained. "Chris has been riding all her life, and she raised Belle from a foal, right on our ranch. For you, a gelding is the best choice. Later, when you've had a lot more experience, you can think about getting a mare."

"Okay," Serena said cheerfully. "As long as the gelding is a palomino."

We left the shed where the bidding was going on and walked out to the corrals where the rest of the horses waited.

All five of us scanned the mass of horseflesh, looking for the golden coat and blond mane of a palomino. We saw lots of pintos, both piebalds, who are black and white, and skewbalds, brown and white. There were plenty of Appaloosas too, some with all-over spots, others with the splashes just on their hindquarters. Some were almost solid in color, but their striped hoofs and the white circles around their eyes marked them as one of the most popular breeds in the West.

I saw lots of brown horses, every shade of gray, plus plenty of bays, duns, buckskins and roans, and my own favorite, chestnuts. Belle has that rich coppery coat, with a slightly lighter reddish-brown mane.

Where were the palominos?

"There's one!" Serena pointed to the back of the largest corral.

"I see another," Mrs. Chang said. "It's tied over by that horse van."

"Does that mean it's for sale?" Serena asked.

"We'll find out." Dad headed for the van.

I kept looking for more golden coats as we walked over but didn't see any. Only two palominos in the entire group? Usually you'd see a few more.

The horse tied to the van stood quiet and calm but he held his head up and his ears forward, meaning he was alert and interested in what was going on around him. He was a nice size for Serena, just over fifteen hands, and I liked the curve of his neck and the clean, straight legs.

"Oooh, he's *beautiful*," Serena whispered.

"Don't get your hopes up, honey," Mr. Chang said. "He's almost too good looking and is probably priced way beyond what you can afford."

Serena was paying for her horse with the money she'd earned by helping to fix up her family's ranch. It was pretty run-down when they bought it and

35

Louise Ladd

they'd worked hard all summer long, Serena included, to whip it into shape.

The palomino sniffed us with curiosity as we approached him. The first thing Dad did was to study him from all angles. "Nice topline," he said. "Good chest, hindquarters not camped out, but he's a bit on the thin side."

"I'll feed him plenty of oats and fatten him up," Serena said.

A short man wearing dusty jeans and a red-checked shirt came up to us. "You folks interested in Dandelion?" He slapped him lightly on the rump and the horse did a little sidestep.

"Might be," Dad said. "How old is he?"

"Eight, in peak condition. Here, let me show you." He opened Dandelion's mouth so Dad could see he was speaking the truth. You can tell a horse's age pretty close by checking his teeth.

"Does he like to jump?" Dad asked, winking at Serena.

"Sure does," the man said. "He's an all-around horse, a good cow pony, but he loves to jump too."

Dad asked a number of other questions, ran his hands down the legs to see if they were sound, then had the man lead him around a bit so he could watch the way he moved. He wouldn't say so out loud, but I could tell he was impressed.

I was too. Dandelion appeared to be such a nice horse that Serena probably couldn't afford him. I waited for Dad to ask the question.

36

The Perfect Horse

Finally he did. "How much are you hoping to get for him?"

The man took off his hat and scratched his head. "He's worth a lot more than I'll probably get, but I'd be happy to settle for around a thousand."

"A thousand dollars!" Serena gasped. "But I only have five hundred saved up!"

"Oh?" The man looked at her. "So he's to be your horse then, is he?" He thought for a moment, his eyes squinting into the distance. "Of course, I said I'd like to get more, but then I might have to settle for less, too. You never can tell with auctions."

"Why isn't he in the corral with the other horses?" Mrs. Chang asked.

"I wanted to pretty him up a bit." The man nodded at a table with a currycomb, brushes, and other grooming equipment on it. It was clear from the shine on Dandelion's coat they'd been put to good use.

"Why are you selling him?" Mr. Chang asked.

"I can't afford to winter him over. Hate to part with him, though."

He slapped Dandelion on the rump again and the palomino laid his ears back. That told me that while the man claimed he liked the horse, the horse didn't like him. It also showed that while he seemed to have a calm nature, he also had a bit of spunk in him.

"Well, thank you," Dad said. "We have a number of others to look at."

The man nodded and we strolled away. After giving a few other horses a once-over, Dad stopped at the corral fence near the only other palomino.

Compared to Dandelion, this horse was a sorry sight. It was clear he was well past his prime. He had two bowed tendons, mutton withers and was swaybacked. His head drooped and so did his tail.

"Poor old thing," Serena said.

"We're not interested in charity cases," her father said. "We're looking for the right horse for you."

"And Dandelion is *it!*" Serena said. "*If* I can afford him."

"Well now," Dad said. "He's a good-looker, but . . ."

"But what?" Serena asked.

"I'm not sure." Dad spoke slowly. "Can't put my finger on it, but I'm not sold one hundred percent. First, I don't know the owner, never saw him before, and there's something about him . . ."

"But we're interested in the horse, not the man," Mrs. Chang said. She seemed to have fallen for Dandelion too.

"Sometimes you learn a lot about a horse by knowing the owner. I'd like to ask around, see if anyone here can tell me about him."

"Okay," Serena said. "But I'm going to bid for Dandelion anyway. He's beautiful! He's perfect! And if I can afford him, I'm going to buy him!"

chapter four

"Serena," Mr. Chang said, "don't get carried away. Bart is the expert on horses and you should listen to his advice."

"Yes, I know." She said to my dad, "I'm sorry, Mr. Bradley. But if you don't find anything wrong with him, and the price isn't too high, Dandelion is the horse I want."

"Well now, I think I got that message pretty clear," Dad said, grinning. "Let me wander around a bit, talk to some friends and see what I can find out. Why don't you ask when the palomino will come up for bidding?"

We did as he suggested and found out we wouldn't have too long to wait, under an hour. We sat in the shed, watching the other horses being sold off. They'd bring in a group at a time, then the owner would walk them around one by one while the crowd made their bids.

I saw Dad talking to a number of different people. Finally he came over to us. We waited to hear what he had to say.

"The owner's name is Sawyer, but no one knows him personally. He brought two big trailer loads down from his place up in Canada. He's not a talkative sort, but the impression is he's a sharp breeder. People are impressed with the quality of his stock, and he might get a good price for them."

"Oh." Serena looked down at her hands. She'd bitten her nails down almost to the knuckles. "Then I probably can't afford Dandelion."

"Maybe, maybe not," Dad said. "Sawyer will only get what people are willing to pay, and some aren't too keen on buying from a man whose reputation we don't know, and one who'll return to Canada right away."

"It sounds like you agree with them, Bart," Mr. Chang said.

"What I'd like to do is see Serena ride that palomino before we make up our minds," Dad said. "See how he goes with a young rider on him."

"Great!" Serena jumped up. "Come on!"

We followed her outside and found Sawyer standing near a line of horses waiting to go into the auction ring.

"Why sure," Sawyer said when Dad made his request. "I'd be happy to give her a chance to try out Dandelion. The problem is, there isn't time. This lot of mine is up next, then it's his turn."

Dad frowned. "I'd rather not bid on the horse until I see her ride him."

Sawyer shook his head. "I don't blame you, but what can I do? If you'd asked earlier ..." He glanced at Serena. "Don't worry, miss, there are plenty of other good horses around. I'm sure you'll find one you like."

Serena bit her lip, then turned away. I followed her over to where Dandelion was waiting quietly in the corral. He tossed his head and whinnied when he saw us.

"He knows me already!" Serena said. "Oh Chris, I *have* to buy him."

"He sure has a lot of spirit, doesn't he?" I admired the bright gleam in his eye and the proud way he held his head. "And since he's only just under sixteen hands—perfect for you, but kind of small for most people—maybe you won't have too much competition for him."

"Wow, Chris, I sure hope you're right."

Dad and Serena's parents came up to us. "Let's watch the bidding on Sawyer's first group," Dad suggested. "Might tell us something."

We went back inside the shed. Many of Sawyer's were good, ordinary cutting horses, and some were much better than average. There wasn't a loser in the group. They all went for prices lower than Dad expected, though.

"You see, Serena," Dad explained, "a breeder's

reputation counts for a lot. Sawyer would get more money if he were selling where he's known."

"Then why isn't he?" Mrs. Chang asked. "Why come all the way down from Canada?"

Mr. Chang answered her. "It costs a lot to feed a herd of horses over the winter months, and you don't get any work out of them in return. And Canada's winter lasts longer than ours."

"You're right, Lew," Dad agreed. "That could be *one* reason."

"Sawyer already told us that's why he's selling," Mr. Chang said.

I was getting the feeling that even Mr. Chang was beginning to side with Serena, or at least wanting to please her. He sounded like he wasn't as interested in Dad's caution as he was before.

"There he is!" Serena pointed as Dandelion stepped smartly into the ring. "Dad, you *have* to bid for him!"

Mr. Chang glanced from her to the horse to Dad. "Bart, you said that Sawyer agreed to give us a written guarantee."

"Yes, but that's only a piece of paper, not worth much unless you know the seller will back it up."

"Well, I'll make a low bid, then we'll see what happens," Mr. Chang decided.

"*Thanks, Dad!*" Serena threw her arms around him and he hugged her back.

Then there he was, the first horse up, that pretty golden coat gleaming as he was led around the ring, stepping smart on strong legs that would carry him easy over rough country. He sure did look like the perfect horse for Serena.

The bidding opened at three hundred dollars, then went up in bumps of 25's. We weren't the only ones impressed by Dandelion. In no time it was up to four hundred dollars. Serena bit off a nail that wasn't even there anymore.

"$425," someone said.

"$450," Mr. Chang said.

"$475," someone else bid.

Mr. Chang said, "$500."

There was a pause. Serena and I held our breath. Then I heard, "$525."

"$525," the auctioneer repeated. "Anyone want to bid $550?"

"Dad! Please! Could you loan me the extra money?" Serena begged. "I'll pay you back—"

"$550," Mr. Chang said quickly.

Another pause. I'd plain quit breathing altogether.

"$575," from the other side of the ring.

Mr. Chang glanced at Serena's pinched face. "$600."

Pause.

"I have $600," the auctioneer said. "Do I hear $625?" Pause. "$600, going once—"

"$625," a voice called.

"Do I hear $650?" the auctioneer asked.

Mr. Chang shot Serena another quick look. Her eyes were full of panic. "$650," he said.

"Do I hear $675? Anyone want to give me $675?" the auctioneer asked.

Pause.

"$650 going once," the auctioneer chanted. "Going twice . . ." He waited. Bang! went the gavel. "Sold for $650 to the gentleman in the blue shirt."

"That's us!" Serena screamed, jumping up and hugging her dad so hard around the neck he almost choked. "He's mine! Dandelion is mine! Thanks, Dad! Thank you! Thank you! Thank you!"

People around us laughed, but Serena didn't even notice. "Come on! Let's go see my horse!"

She ran out of the shed and we followed almost as fast. I was the only one who noticed that Dad was shaking his head slightly. We found the person who did the paperwork and collected the money. We didn't see Sawyer, since he was still inside with the rest of his horses.

While Dad and Mr. Chang took care of business, Serena raced over to Dandelion. When he saw her galloping toward him, he snorted and danced back a bit, startled.

"Easy, Serena," I called. "Don't scare him like that."

She slowed down right away and walked quietly up to him. He gave her a sniff, then she remembered the trick. Leaning forward, she huffed her breath into his nose. Dandelion pulled back a second, then huffed at her.

"Oooh, he smells like hay," she said, giggling.

"He's one of the prettiest horses I ever saw," Mrs. Chang said, joining us. "You're a lovely boy, aren't you?" she asked, stroking his neck.

We fussed over him some more until Dad and Mr. Chang came over, then, with Serena floating on several layers of clouds, we led him to our horse trailer.

That's when we ran into some trouble. Dandelion didn't want to be loaded into the van. He backed, he sidestepped, he swung his hindquarters around and shook his head. He even reared up a few times, but Dad had a good grip on his lead rope and pulled him down real smart.

"You can't blame him, poor thing," Serena said. "He's just been driven all the way down from Canada. He probably thinks he's going to have to take another long ride."

"That's right," Mrs. Chang agreed. "Don't worry, Dandelion, it's only a short trip home." She reached up to pat his shoulder but he swung his head around and glared at her and she quickly changed her mind.

"Dad, that's all it is, isn't it?" I asked, suddenly worried.

"Could be," he said slowly, studying the horse. "Let's hope so. Lew, hand me a rope."

"You're not going to whip him, are you?" Serena asked, scared. She'd been watching Dandelion's performance, tense as a coiled rattler.

"Of course not." Dad gave her an easy smile. He

took the short rope and gave one end each to Mr. and Mrs. Chang, passing it behind Dandelion's hindquarters. Then he took hold of the halter and spoke to the horse in a calm, soothing voice.

When the palomino was quiet, Dad said, "Now, as I lead him in, Mai and Lew, pull the rope toward the trailer. Keep a steady pressure on his rump, but make sure you don't saw it back and forth."

With the Changs on either side nudging the horse from behind with the rope and Dad gently guiding from the front, Dandelion walked up the ramp and inside with no more fuss.

Mr. Chang quickly closed the doors and wiped the dust and sweat off his face. "Well, Serena, you've got yourself a horse, and a dandy one at that!"

Now that the horse was safely loaded, Serena relaxed. "Dandy! That's what I'll call him. Isn't that the perfect name for the perfect horse?"

Dad started to say something, then changed his mind.

"It's a great name, Serena," I said. "It sure suits him. He's a Dandy all right."

"I can't wait to get home and ride him!"

"You'll probably want to let him settle down a bit first," Dad said. "He's a little . . . over-excited right now."

"Who can blame him?" Mrs. Chang asked. "After all he's been through recently."

Thump! Thump! Thump!

47

Dandy was kicking the trailer.

Dad and I glanced at each other with a flash of worry.

Then I said to Serena, "Congratulations! You've got yourself one beautiful horse!"

I wished I felt as sure as I sounded.

chapter five

With Dandy so restless in the trailer, we didn't stop to eat our lunch but passed out the sandwiches and drinks in the car as Mr. Chang drove home.

No one mentioned the thumps we heard from time to time through the open windows. The Changs had decided Dandy hated the trailer because of the trip from Canada. I hoped they were right. Dad ignored the thumps too and talked about cattle and Colorado ranching with Mr. Chang.

When we turned into the Lazy B, Mr. Chang parked by a small pasture.

"I wanted to show Dandy his stall," Serena said. "It's so big and nice, and I cleaned every inch of it."

"It's best to give him a little room to run first," Dad said. "He's been cooped up for a while."

Thump! Thump! Dandy seemed to agree.

Unloading him was no problem at all. Dandy almost shot out of that trailer. The moment he was turned loose, he took off, seeming to glory in the space and freedom.

"Wow, he's so beautiful," Serena said. "I can't believe he's mine."

"He sure can run," I said, watching the smooth muscles rippling under the golden coat.

"How soon can I ride him?" she asked Dad.

"When he settles down a bit," he said. "Maybe later today, maybe tomorrow. Well, we'd better get going, Chris. Chores are waiting at home."

The Changs said thanks, and thanks again, waving as we drove off.

The Double Diamond was pretty quiet, since most of the guests check out on Saturday morning. Those who were staying for another week were all out on the trail, except for Mr. Harris, the retired rodeo rider. He was in his rocker on the porch, as usual, watching hawks wheeling in the deep blue sky and the sun glowing on the mountain peaks.

I thought about heading for my cabin and getting a start on the weekend homework before the riders got back and I had to help turn out their horses, but decided to stop by the porch and tell Mr. Harris the news first.

"Hi," I said, perching on the railing near him.

"Guess what, Mr. Harris? We bought a horse for Serena today."

"Is that so?" he asked, not exactly interested. In the old days he would have asked a thousand questions.

I told him all about Dandy and the auction, hoping to raise a spark of interest. He listened politely but that was all. I wished I could ask him what was bothering him so much, but I didn't want to appear nosy.

Finally I went inside the house, looking for Anna and Red Wing. I knew they'd like to hear about Dandy. I found them both steaming-mad in the kitchen, giving Drew a going-over. Through the screen door, I saw Monster out under the spruce tree, chewing on a hunk of meat.

"You know that dog is not allowed in the kitchen," Anna was saying, her fury barely under rein. "We run a business here. Do you want the health department to close us down?"

"No, ma'am." Drew kept his eyes on his boots.

"That dog's a thief, plain and simple," Red Wing said. "And he's too smart for his own good. Does he steal the stew beef? No! The hamburger? No! The leftover chicken? No! He takes the best roast, the one I was planning to serve for dinner tonight!"

"Yes, ma'am," Drew said, not looking up.

"It's time you taught that pup his manners," Anna said. "You know what your father will say if he hears of this!"

"Yes, ma'am." Drew glanced up. "*Will* he hear of it?"

Anna and Red Wing looked at each other. Finally Red Wing said, "I'm no blabbermouth."

Anna sighed. "Not if you go out there and take that meat away from your dog. He shouldn't be enjoying stolen food."

"I already tried," Drew said. "You saw me. He just runs off before I can get close to him."

"I think it's too late," I said, pointing. As I spoke, Monster gulped down the last mouthful and ambled off around the house.

Red Wing shook her head and turned back to the stove. Anna sighed again and said, "Go find him and tie him up in the barn. I don't want to see Monster again today."

Drew slunk out the kitchen door, muttering, "His name is Star." But he was careful to make sure his mom couldn't hear him. I followed, my excitement over Serena's new horse forgotten.

"Hey, it's okay," I said as we went down the back steps. "He's only a puppy. He'll learn."

"I've been trying to teach him," Drew said. "I'm working on 'sit' and 'stay' and 'come' but he doesn't listen half the time."

"He's still a baby," I said. "He'll catch on pretty soon."

"That's not all that's bothering me." Drew kicked a stone. Hard. "You remember what Dad said. He won't have a useless, do-nothing dog around. What kind of job can I train Star to do? The only

52

thing he's good at is fetching sticks and balls. How many ranchers need a dog who can drop sticks at their feet?"

"Maybe he has talents we don't know about yet," I said, trying to cheer him up.

"Well, if he does, he's sure keeping it a secret."

"He probably gets his retrieving instincts from his mother." She was a black Labrador. "And—judging by his size—it's sure beginning to look like his father was that Newfoundland, like the vet suspected. What are Newfies good at?"

"I looked them up in the library," Drew said. "They're used for retrieving too, especially in the water, but they can also pull carts and sleds."

"There you go!" I snapped my fingers. "We can hook Monster up to a sled this winter and he can pull the little buckaroos around."

While we talked, we both kept looking, trying to spot the puppy. When we went around the corner of the house, we finally saw him. He was sitting on the porch, leaning against Mr. Harris' legs, gazing up at him with a doggy smile.

Mr. Harris was rubbing the pup's ears and talking to him. We couldn't hear what he was saying, but he was telling Monster something important, his faded blue eyes more lively than usual.

We crept up carefully, hoping to catch the puppy before he could run off again. We didn't really *try* to overhear Mr. Harris, but we couldn't help it.

". . . Yup, Monster, she was a good friend, one of the best. All my life I waited for the right lady to come along and suddenly there she was. Oh, the times we had together, while it lasted. We'd dance and we'd laugh ... Now, take the time she talked me into going bowling. What a sight I was! I'd roll that ball down the lane, and never could get it to go all the way to the pins. Every dang ball landed in the gutter, and each time we laughed harder and harder ..."

He stopped speaking. He also stopped rubbing the pup's ears so Monster yipped, meaning, "Go on."

After a minute Mr. Harris resumed rubbing. "Yup, I waited all my life, then we only had each other for six months ... six months of sunshine and then ... she was gone ... At least she went peacefully ... in her sleep ... Three months ago yesterday, it was ... half the time I knew her ..."

Drew and I glanced at each other and, without a word, turned and tiptoed away. We'd have to wait and catch Monster after Mr. Harris was finished with him.

Now we knew where Mr. Harris' spark had gone. Into the grave, with the lady he'd waited for all his life.

Serena called right after supper, just as I was headed for the cabin to start my homework. The trail riders had come in shortly after we left Monster and Mr. Harris on the porch. We unsaddled, checked the horses over and turned them out to pasture, then Anna asked me to give Red Wing a

54

hand in the kitchen until her helper showed up. I didn't mind—I figured I might as well do my homework all in one big swoop that night.

"Can you come over right away, Chris?" Serena asked when I picked up the phone. "Dad says Dandy has calmed down enough for me to ride him!"

"Well, I was going to—"

"Please, Chris! You have to be here! You taught me not to be afraid of horses, and you taught me to ride. You have to watch me on my very own horse for the very first time!"

I grinned. "Sure, I'll saddle up Belle and be there in just a little while."

"Bring your dad too. I want him to watch me ride my perfect horse."

"Okay. See you in half an hour."

The sky was still plenty light, although the sun was low enough to be hidden behind one of the high mountains that circle our valley. Dad and I rode down to the Lazy B, taking a trail that led directly to the ranch, instead of following the winding road.

Dandy was in the corral, saddled and ready to go. Both he and Serena were dancing with impatience.

"I thought you'd never get here!" Serena said. Her family, including her brothers, greeted us a little more politely. "Dad wants me to stay in the corral but I think we should be allowed out in the pasture."

"One step at a time," Dad said. "You've shown a

lot of good sense this summer, Serena. That's partly why you've turned into such a good rider so quickly. Today the corral, tomorrow the pasture."

"Oh, all right." She climbed over the fence and walked up to Dandy, speaking to him softly. He snorted but stood still while she mounted. "See how well trained he is?" she asked from the saddle.

"You look great on him!" I said. She did, too. Being on the small side like me, she fit him perfectly—or he fit her. "Okay, start him out nice and easy."

She touched his sides and he quickly moved into a fast walk. He was showing a lot more energy than he had that morning at the auction, but maybe that was to be expected, now that his long trip was over and he was home.

He didn't want to stay in a slow jog when the time came. Serena had her hands full keeping him from breaking into a lope, but he obeyed her for the most part. She kept him circling the corral, moving into faster gaits. Mostly that was his idea, rather than hers.

"Rein him in, Serena," Dad called. "Make him listen to you. Show him who's boss."

She tried and Dandy slowed a little.

Mr. Chang leaned on the fence next to Dad. "What do you think, Bart? Can she handle him? He seemed a lot quieter this morning at the auction."

"I've been thinking about that," Dad said. "It's been bothering me that Sawyer was grooming this one particular horse this morning. I noticed that he didn't give the same attention to all of his horses."

I glanced at Dad in surprise. "I didn't realize that."

Dad grinned. "You haven't been around as long as I have, honey. I was wondering why, but I figured that since this horse was so special looking, Sawyer wanted to make sure he was at his best, to fetch the top price."

"Sure, that makes sense," I said.

"It wasn't until this afternoon that I began to wonder if Sawyer was up to something else."

"Do you mean because we had so much trouble loading Dandy into the trailer?" Mr. Chang asked.

"Lots of horses don't like trailers, for lots of reasons. But I saw a gradual change come over this palomino. He was slowly getting more active—he sure fought the trailer harder than I expected, for one thing."

"But what does grooming him have to do with anything?" I asked.

"It's an old trick," Dad said, his mouth grim. "And one I should have thought of before it was too late."

Serena flew past us, just barely keeping Dandy from breaking into an all-out run.

"Pull him in, Serena," Mr. Chang called. "Make him slow down." She tried, with only a little success.

"What trick?" I asked.

"If you take a horse out and ride him long enough

and hard enough," Dad said, "sooner or later he's going to get tired."

"And when he's tired," I said, catching on, "he's going to seem like a quiet, gentle horse. And if you give him a good grooming, you can wipe away the sweat and other signs that he's just had a lot of exercise. Is that right, Dad?"

"That's exactly it, Chris." Dad patted me on the back. "You got it."

Mr. Chang watched Serena flash past us again. "Are you saying that Sawyer sold us a horse that's dangerous?"

"Not necessarily dangerous, but he's a lot of horse for your little girl to handle."

"That lowdown rat!" Mr. Chang's face turned red with anger. "I'd like to wring Sawyer's neck!"

"But, Dad," I pointed out. "He *did* say Serena should look for another horse—I remember he told her there were plenty of good ones to choose from."

"So he said, but that was after he saw how much she wanted Dandelion. It was written on her face plain as could be. He knew we'd bid up the price." Dad called out to her as she went by again. "Ease him down now, Serena! See if you can slow him a bit."

She heard him and tried to pull Dandy back. He fought her, but she managed to slow him a notch.

"Look, Dad, she can handle him. Sure, maybe it will take some time before—"

Dandy sped up. He ran straight for the corral fence. He didn't stop. He jumped the fence, with Serena clinging to his back!

chapter six

When Dandy landed on the far side of the fence, Serena lost her stirrups but managed to stay in the saddle. She bent over low, pulling on the reins to bring his head down, but he was too strong for her.

They were halfway up the drive, headed for the main road, before Dad and I could scramble onto our horses. Belle leaped into a run from a standing start.

Dad was right beside me as we raced after the runaway horse.

"Hang on tight, Serena! We're coming!" I shouted even though I knew she couldn't hear me.

Dandy and Serena disappeared around a bend in the drive. We had to catch them before they hit the main road. There wasn't much traffic, but all it took was one car or truck and—I didn't want to think about it.

We rounded the bend and I saw Serena slip sideways in the saddle. Without stirrups, she dropped the reins and grabbed the saddlehorn to keep from falling. Dandy was running full-out like he never planned to stop.

The drive took another bend to the left but the palomino kept going straight, headed right for a pasture fence.

Dandy sailed over the fence. Serena clung to him for a moment, then she was in the air. She landed on her side and rolled over and over—then lay still.

Her horse kept running, a streak of gold through a herd of black cattle.

I pulled Belle up just short of the fence and jumped down from the saddle. Dad was right behind me.

"Serena, are you okay?" I yelled. "Serena, answer me!"

Did she turn her head slightly or did I imagine it?

Dad and I climbed over the fence and ran to her. Just then Mr. Chang and Tommy drove up in the jeep.

"Serena!" I dropped to my knees beside her. "Are you all right? Talk to me!"

She lay on her back, her eyes closed, but as I watched, they flickered open. She blinked a few times, then focused on my face. "I'm sorry," she whispered. "I—I tried . . ."

"You did great," I said, taking her hand. "You stuck on that horse much longer than I ever thought you could."

She gave me the teensiest smile.

Then Dad and Mr. Chang took over, checking her for injuries. The rest of the family arrived and everyone hovered around her. Mrs. Chang kept swallowing, trying not to cry, but a few tears spilled out anyway.

Finally Dad said, "Nothing's broken, and there's no concussion but you'll have a few good bruises to show off, Serena, including a real shiner."

Serena's left eyebrow was swollen and already beginning to turn color. Dad was right—she was going to have one heck of a black eye.

"Hey, you'll be a hero in school, Serena," I said. "And you sure have a whopper of a story to tell."

"Dandy! Where is he?" She tried to sit up and I gave her a boost. She winced when I touched her back. She was going to be one mighty sore girl for a while.

I glanced around the pasture and saw no sign of the palomino. "He probably didn't get too far. I'll go look for him, after we get you home."

"When you find him," Mr. Chang growled. "Keep him out of my sight. I'd like to turn him into dog meat!"

"Dad!" Serena turned pale.

"I'm just kidding," he said. "But he sure gave us all a real scare."

"It was my fault. I couldn't control him. Please,

Chris, go find him now," she begged. "He might have hurt himself."

I remembered how worried I was when my Belle was terrified into running away not long before. "Okay, I will."

While Serena's family helped her into the car, I mounted Belle and rode down to the gate. Letting myself into the pasture, I followed Dandy's track across the grass and into a pine grove that climbed up a slope.

And there he was, drinking from a clear brook that spilled down from a tiny waterfall. He was lathered up but he still looked darn pretty, and not the least bit sorry.

Now that he'd had his fun, he let me ride up to him and take the reins. I got down and checked him out. He stood quietly while I went over his legs, even nuzzling my neck when I inspected his left front hoof.

"There's nothing wrong with you, Dandy," I scratched his pale blond mane. "You're just too much horse for Serena right now. That's your only problem."

I led him back to the barn, tied both horses to a post, and went inside the house where I found everyone else had come to the same conclusion.

Except Serena. "No! You can't send him back," she was saying, "He's mine!"

"Lew," Dad said. "Sawyer is halfway to Canada by now. Even if you track him down, you may never see the money again. Anyone who would pull a shady trick like that has a bunch of others in his bag. Your best bet is to sell the horse to someone around here, an experienced rider who can handle him."

"No, don't sell him! Please!" Serena said. "I'll work hard and learn to be a better rider. Please let me keep him!"

"All right, everyone," her mother said. "That's enough. We can decide what to do with Dandy tomorrow, or even next week. Right now, I want Serena to soak in a hot tub, then go to bed. It's been a long day and it's getting late."

I glanced out the window. It was almost dark out.

"You're right, Mai," Dad said. "Come on, Chris, we'd better head home while we can still see the trail."

"Okay," I said. "Good night, Serena, and don't worry, we'll fix this right somehow."

Sunday is always a busy day on the Double Diamond. That's when the new guests arrive and we have to help them settle in. Most people are eager to hit the trail right away, and the wranglers, with help from Drew and me as junior wranglers, have to figure out which horse and saddle are best suited to each guest.

We also help out around the ranch house, carrying luggage and showing people to their cabins. This week, the last full week before Labor Day and the start of school in most parts of the country, we had a lot more kids than usual, ranging from tiny babies up through high school.

Drew's Monster was the happiest pup you ever saw. He thought all these new kids had been sent just for his pleasure. He dashed from one family to another, greeting each kid with wet doggy kisses and a wildly wagging tail.

"Look, Mommy, . . . bear!" Jenny, a two-year-old, squealed when she spotted him.

Like I said before, Monster, young as he was, was already the size of a half-grown cub, and with his fat, black furry body and his short little snout, he could easily pass for a small bear if you're only two years old.

I noticed that Mr. Harris, rocking on the front porch, had perked up a bit as he watched the puppy racing around. As I led one family to the house to sign in with Anna, I saw him actually grinning when a little boy tried to "ride" Monster. They both ended up rolling around in the grass and it was hard to tell who was having more fun.

I called Serena at lunchtime. "How are you feeling?" I asked.

"Well, the little toe on my right foot doesn't ache," she said. "That's about the only spot that doesn't."

"I know what you mean. I've been tossed off more than once," I said. "The first day after is always the worst. Sometimes an ice pack helps."

"*An* ice pack?" She laughed. "Mom has me covered with cold packs, top to bottom. It's a full-time job just switching them around."

"Lucky you. Maybe you'll get out of school tomorrow."

As soon as I said it, I remembered the homework I hadn't started yet. In addition to math, science and English, I had a fat book, *Little Women*, which I had to start reading and write a report on by the end of the month. When Mrs. Brown assigned it to me, I tried to switch to a book about horses, but she made me take this one. Last night, after I got home from the Lazy B, I started it but fell asleep on the second page.

Oh well, there was still tonight. I'd get right to my homework after supper.

"Mom wants me to stay home," Serena said, "but I want to go to school. If I get behind, how will I ever catch up?"

"Maybe "Homework" Brown will understand," I said.

"Not unless I broke a zillion bones," she said. "And I couldn't even manage to break just one."

I was glad to hear her sounding so cheerful. It gave me the courage to ask the question I'd been dreading the answer to. "Serena, you're not . . . scared of getting on a horse again, are you? Sometimes when people get thrown . . . and you just got beyond your fear of horses anyway . . ."

"I woke up wondering the same thing," she said. "So I made my brother Matt saddle up his pinto, Tom-Tom, and even though I could hardly move, he helped me on and guess what?"

"What?"

66

"I walked Tom-Tom around the corral for almost half an hour, just to make sure I was over my fear."

"Good for you!" I wondered if I'd be able to do the same, knowing full well how sore she felt, and not ever being afraid of horses in my life.

"The only thing I'm scared of is losing Dandy," she said.

"What did your dad say this morning?"

"When he first saw my black eye, he told me he was going to call the dog food factory." She caught her breath for a moment. "I knew he wasn't serious, but after that Mom made everyone promise not to discuss it for a few days, until we calmed down. Right now, Dandy's in the pasture, grazing as nice and quiet as could be. Maybe he was just wild yesterday, do you think?"

"I wish I could say yes, Serena, but to be honest I have to say no. He's too much for you to handle. At least for now. Maybe by spring—"

"Spring! I want to ride my own horse *now*!"

An idea came to me. "Let me talk to Dad. Maybe ... No, I won't say anything until I find out what he thinks."

"What?" Serena demanded. "Tell me!"

"I can't—yet. I'll let you know on the way to school tomorrow morning. That's *if* Dad says yes."

"Are you going to keep me wondering all day and night?"

"Sure." I grinned. "It will give you something to think about besides your aches. Listen, I've got to get back to work. See you tomorrow."

"Chris!" she wailed.

"Tomorrow," I promised.

I was kept busy with the new guests all day but right after supper I headed out of the dining room, certain I was going straight to the cabin and plow into my homework.

On the way, I passed through the lounge and guess what movie was just starting to play on the VCR? *Little Women!* The big, fat—horseless—book I was supposed to read and write a report on.

Well, how could I pass up a chance like that? I thought of the hours and hours it would save if I watched it instead of read it. Mrs. Brown would never know the difference.

I plunked myself down in a comfortable chair, sure that I'd made the right decision.

Boy, can I be wrong sometimes.

chapter seven

"Okay, what's your idea and what did your dad say about it?" Serena demanded when we stopped to pick her up the next morning.

She'd climbed into the car moving as slow as a frozen river, due to her bruises, but that didn't stop her from asking the question before she even got around to saying, "hi."

"Wow, look at your eye," Drew said. "What a shiner!"

"How are you feeling, Serena?" Anna asked as she turned the station wagon toward the road down the mountain.

"I'm a little stiff but I'll be okay, Mrs. Diamond," she said politely. "Thank you for asking." Then she grabbed my wrist. "Chris, tell me right this minute."

"Well, Dad and I think we have the perfect horse for you," I began.

"I already own the perfect horse!" she wailed. "I just can't ride him yet!"

"Let me explain first." I peeled her fingers away before they cut off all the blood that was supposed to feed my hand. "Come fall, after we sell this year's crop of calves, we drive the rest of the cattle to their winter range."

"What do *cows* have to do with this?" she asked.

"Wait a minute, I'm getting there. After that, when the weather gets cold, not as many guests come to the ranch—at least not until Christmas vacation."

"What do *guests* have to do with this?"

"They both have to do with horses." I was trying to be patient with her. "We don't need a lot of horses to tend the cattle, and there aren't many guests to ride them, so we only keep a few horses on the ranch, just the ones we need. We sell some and take the others down the mountain to the winter pastures the Diamonds rent."

"Chris," she said. "Tell me your idea, *please*!"

"I am. One of the horses Dad was planning to sell is Eagle, the horse you've been riding. There's nothing wrong with him, except he's a little too tame for the really advanced riders, and a little too zippy for a lot of the intermediates, so Dad was planning to replace him anyway."

"What does that mean?" she asked.

"He's perfect for you. Just enough of a challenge, but not too much to handle. You can learn a lot on him—and he loves to jump, don't forget. So how would you like to buy Eagle from us?"

"*Eagle*? He's the ugliest horse I've ever seen!" she said. "Besides, I can't afford two horses. And I still owe Dad a hundred and fifty dollars for Dandy."

"This will fix that problem too," I said. "You got a real bargain on Dandy, and Dad is willing to pay you what he thinks he's worth—a thousand dollars!"

"A—a thousand. . . . ?" Serena blinked.

"Yup. That way you can pay back your father what you owe *and* have enough left over to buy Eagle. Dad is willing to let him go for $350, although he'd probably get more if he sold him elsewhere."

In fact, though I didn't tell Serena, Eagle would fetch a whole lot more than that.

She thought for a second, then sat up straight, wincing from the sudden movement and the pain it caused her. "Wait a minute! I have to *sell Dandy*?!"

"Only for a while. Dad will sell him back to you anytime you're ready to take him on, maybe as soon as next spring."

"*Sell my perfect horse?*" Her eyes were huge with horror.

"Just for a while. Dad and Andy will ride him this winter, give him some training, and we think you'll both be ready for each other by spring, probably."

71

Louise Ladd

"*And buy Eagle? The ugliest horse in the world?*"
Drew twisted around in the front seat to look back at her. "He's not ugly. He's an Appaloosa."

"I hate all those spots—and they're only on his rump, not even all over. And he's a boring color."

"He's a blue roan. His hair is black and white mixed together. That's not so boring," Drew said.

"Yes it is." She sat back, ignoring her bruises. "Sell my beautiful palomino . . . and buy an ugly, boring horse . . ."

"He's not boring to ride," I said. "You enjoy him."
She gave me a look, but didn't say anything.

Anna broke the silence. "There's an old, old saying, Serena: 'A good horse can never be of a bad color.' There's a lot of wisdom in that thought."

Still Serena said nothing.

I was disappointed. I thought I'd come up with a great idea, but I hadn't counted on her thinking Eagle was ugly. To me, all horses are beautiful, because they're horses.

Just before we reached the bus stop, Serena finally said in a small voice, "Thank you for your offer. I can see you and your dad are trying to do me a favor, Chris, and I appreciate it. But sell Dandy . . . I'll have to think about it for a while."

"Sure," I said. "There's plenty of time to decide."

Anna pulled up at the bus stop and Serena began to crawl out of the car. She couldn't move faster than one muscle at a time.

"Look at that eye!" "Wow!" "What happened to you?" the little kids asked when they spotted her.

72

The Perfect Horse

Both handsome, blond Hatcher twins—to my surprise—rushed over. Zeke and Josh helped her from the car, leading her to the side of the road where the bus would stop.

"What did you do this weekend?" Zeke asked. "Play football with the Dallas Cowboys?"

"Or the Chicago Bears?" Josh added.

Then—to my double surprise—Serena smiled up at both of them. "In fact, it was the San Francisco Forty-Niners."

Well! Let me tell you, that was just the beginning. It soon became clear I didn't have to worry about shy Serena anymore. She talked to the twins all the way into town. That was okay with me, since I still had my science homework to do, but she didn't mind in the least the attention she drew at school too. She told the story over and over, each time making it a little better, until by the end of the day, Dandy had turned into a wild bucking bronco she'd almost managed to tame.

I was glad for her. It's nice to see a butterfly blooming right before your eyes.

I wasn't so lucky. The math and English homework I'd done the night before, when I was half asleep after watching *Little Women*, came back covered with those X's I'd learned to dread. Mrs. Brown had a little "chat" with me in private, and I promised to do better, but, of course, I still spent recess and lunch at my desk.

It was good to get home again when Mrs. Chang finally dropped Drew and me off at the Double Diamond. Monster was on the porch, sitting beside Mr. Harris, who appeared to be telling the pup a long story.

The dog sat quietly listening until Mr. Harris looked up and noticed us. He must have told Monster we'd arrived because, in seconds, Drew and I were smothered in black furry love, muddy paws and all.

As we tried to defend ourselves from the attack, Mr. Harris laughed. He actually laughed out loud! It was a wonder, and all because of one not-so-small puppy.

"Look, Drew," I whispered, nudging him. "Your dad can't say Monster isn't of some use around here. Mr. Harris hasn't been so lively since he arrived."

"That's true," Drew agreed. "But I wonder if Dad thinks cheering up sad people is a real job for a ranch dog."

"Well, he's a *dude* ranch dog, so maybe Andy will give Monster some credit for helping out with the guests."

"Maybe." He tried to sound hopeful, though he knew his father thought a dog should be employed with real work, like old Shep was, rounding up heifers and stray calves.

But Monster had another surprise in store.

That evening Anna was planning a barbecue around the swimming pool, followed by a sing-along, which I always enjoy, so I went straight to the cabin and dug into my homework. (Well, I cheated a little by doing it outside under the aspen trees that surround the log cabin Dad and I share.)

I discovered something. It's a lot faster to solve math problems when you're wide awake. I finished up all my assignments in record time, then fetched Belle from the pasture and we had a good ride before it was time to wash up for supper.

Feeling proud of myself, I almost swaggered over to the swimming pool. A few kids were still splashing around but their mother hustled them out, telling them to go change into dry clothes. The water is heated, but our mountain air gets chilly at night.

Several families were collected around the tables by the shallow end, listening to Andy Diamond tell some of his famous stories about the ranching life. Kids of every size were running around, in and out of the game room, over to the playground and back.

The grown-ups were watching Andy as he showed them how he caught the bull that had broken down the barn door. I stood at the back of the group, enjoying the story I knew almost by heart.

Behind me, over the shrieking, shouting kids, I heard a small splash but didn't pay much attention.

Then I heard Monster's arf-arf-arf, sounding a new note, almost a *look-look-look!* sound.

I glanced behind me. Monster stood at the far end of the swimming pool, barking in panic, his eyes fixed on a small bundle of clothes floating about six feet away in the deep end.

The clothes moved and a face rose out of the water for a second. It was tiny, two-year-old Jenny.

Before I could put my feet in motion, Monster hit the water. He paddled furiously to the bundle and grabbed a piece of shirt with his puppy teeth. Then he turned around and started towing the baby toward the edge of the pool.

"Andy!" I screamed as I ran to the deep end. "Help! Everyone! Help!"

I dove over the side and surfaced next to them. Grabbing the toddler by the pants, I pushed her and Monster to the edge of the water. Moments later, hands reached down and lifted them both out.

As you can guess, there was an awful lot of fuss after that. The baby was fine, but her mother did a good bit of crying before she calmed down. Everyone had seen Monster's rescue and they couldn't get over it. When people tried to thank me, I directed the praise where it was due.

Monster was one happy dog that night. He had all the attention he could ask for, as well as more than a few tastes of barbecued steak and a chunk of chicken or two. But it was the loving he enjoyed best.

Later, after we ate, while Jamie was tuning up his guitar for the sing-along, I saw Drew and his dad talking. Andy Diamond is a fair man, if a bit stubborn at times, and when Andy reached down to give Monster a friendly pat, I figured he'd begun to appreciate Drew's pup for what he was, a people-dog with retriever instincts, and a real addition to the Double Diamond Dude Ranch.

I went to bed feeling good that night. Now, if I could only make Serena understand that—for the moment—the Ugliest Horse in the World was the perfect horse for her.

chapter eight

Serena couldn't make up her mind about Dandy and Eagle. The weeks went by, and still she couldn't decide. In the meantime, Dandy filled out his thin bones on the extra oats she was feeding him, although he'd never be a fat horse, due to being so active.

Mr. Chang and Serena's older brothers tried him out, and while they didn't get thrown, they found him a nuisance. They spent more time keeping him under control than getting their work done. Dandy needed someone with years of horse experience, like Dad or Andy Diamond, to teach him manners.

September rolled along. The dude ranch was still full of guests, but mostly grown-ups, since the kids were back in school.

The Perfect Horse

Mrs. Brown and I had come to an agreement. I did my homework and she didn't keep me in at recess and lunch. That made school easier to get through, since being shut inside all day doesn't come easy to a person like me.

Of course, not having to read that fat book helped. I could do my other assignments and still have time to enjoy life.

Soon after seeing *Little Women* on the VCR, I'd filled out my book report form, so I wouldn't forget the details. I listed my favorite character as Beth, because she died, and checked the box asking if I enjoyed it "yes," because it was a good movie, if a bit slow. Where it asked me to describe one scene, I told about the end, figuring that if Mrs. Brown hadn't read the book yet, I'd save her the bother.

There were a couple of other questions I had no trouble answering, and so I wasn't the tiniest bit worried when I handed in the report along with the other kids in class.

A few days later, Mrs. Brown passed out the graded papers. I was expecting an A, *maybe* a B, and I quickly flipped to the second page where she put the marks. F. A big red F! And a comment: "You were asked to read the book, not watch the movie!"

My face burned and I stuffed the report quickly in the back of my notebook. I glanced around to see if anyone had noticed. They hadn't. Some, including Serena, were smiling—the A people, of course—and a few were frowning. I skimmed

the papers I could see from where I sat. No one got anything lower than a C, at least not that I could tell.

Once I was over the shock, curiosity began to grow. All through class, I sat there wondering, *how did she guess?*

The bell finally rang for recess and, instead of dashing outside like usual, I waited for the others to clear the room, then went up to Mrs. Brown's desk. I just had to know the answer.

"Yes, Chris?" Mrs. Brown said.

"Um ... about the book report ... how could you tell?"

She smiled. "Give me your report and I'll show you."

I dug it out and handed it to her, feeling the blush creeping over my face again at the sight of the F.

"Here's a clue, for instance." She pointed to the question: Describe one detail from the book that you found especially interesting and tell why. "Read your answer to me, Chris."

I read, "One carriage horse was ewe-necked and his forelegs were over at the knee. Another had a bad case of founder. I wondered why those rich people made such poor choices. If I had that kind of money, I'd pay a lot more and get myself really fine horses."

"Do you see anything wrong with your answer?" Mrs. Brown asked.

I shrugged. "It makes sense to me."

"Chris, the carriage horses are never described—in the book—as ewe-necked, whatever that means, nor are forelegs and founder discussed. You *saw* those horses, Chris, you didn't read about them."

"Oh."

"And don't forget, I've been teaching for many years," Mrs. Brown said with another smile. "You're not the first student who has tried to get away with this. By now I think I've seen it all, so if I were you, I wouldn't bother to try to bend the rules again."

"Yes, ma'am." I felt lower than a skunk.

"However," she said, "since it's obvious your attention is captured by horses, in the future I'll try to assign you books that include at least one horse in it. For instance, *National Velvet* is a wonderful story about a horse race, although you might find the accents a challenge to read. Would you like to try it anyway?"

"If it's about a horse, yes, ma'am."

"All right, that will be your next assignment. Now, you'd better hurry or you'll miss recess, and I know how much it means to you." She smiled again.

I was about out the door when she stopped me. "And Chris, they made a terrific movie of *National Velvet*, but I wouldn't advise watching it until after you've read the book."

"Yes, ma'am." I hurried down the hall, wondering how Mrs. Brown had learned to develop X-ray vision. Maybe she was related to Superman. Not that

The Perfect Horse

I wasn't planning to read *National Velvet* too, but what's the harm in watching a good movie? Afterward, of course.

I was a whole lot smarter with Serena than I was with Mrs. Brown. After waiting and waiting for her to come to a decision, I worked up a plan.

She'd been riding "ugly" Eagle whenever she visited the Double Diamond, and I kept thinking she'd begin to want him the more she got used to him. When that didn't happen, I decided to try the opposite.

"Serena," I said when she arrived on a Sunday, "Eagle is being ridden by one of the guests this week." I'd set that up with Maggie, our head wrangler. Fortunately, one of our regulars, Mrs. Hopper, liked Eagle and they were a good match, although she was an expert and could have ridden almost any horse on the ranch.

"But what about my jumping lessons?" Serena asked.

"Marigold, the pinto, likes to jump," I said.

"But she's a beginner's horse," Serena said.

"Why don't you try her anyway and see what you think?"

She agreed, and just as I expected, found Marigold pretty tame and boring after riding Eagle.

The next day I tried her on a different horse, Bandit, who had more zip but hated jumping, balking at the rails half the time. She got real frustrated with him. The following day, it was Spritzer,

83

who had zip and liked to jump but had such a short, choppy stride he was a chore to ride.

It went on like that for a week. Horse after horse, I let her find out for herself that Eagle was the perfect one for her.

Mrs. Hopper went home on Saturday, and Sunday morning Serena showed up in the barn right after breakfast, while I was saddling Belle.

"Do you think Eagle will be used on the trail again this week?" she asked, trying to sound casual.

"I don't know. The new guests haven't arrived yet," I said, just as casual. "We'll have to wait and see which horses they need—or want."

"Well . . . do you think I could ride Eagle this morning anyway? Before the new people get here?"

I looked over at the pasture, where the Appaloosa was grazing. "I'm not sure. Mrs. Hopper gave him a real workout all week long. I overheard Maggie telling Jamie that Eagle deserved a rest, unless one of the guests particularly asked for him."

"Oh . . . okay." She turned away.

I fastened Belle's back girth. "But—maybe I could ask Maggie if you could ride him just for a short while. Say, half an hour?"

"Chris! Would you?" She brightened right up.

"No problem. All she can do is say no." Feeling a little guilty for the trick I was playing on her— but pleased as all get-out because it was working—I went down to the far end of the barn and faked a conference with Maggie. She, of course, was in on the whole plan and after pretending to let me convince her, finally nodded yes.

Serena saw Maggie nod. Before I could walk back with the answer, she'd grabbed a halter and was racing for the pasture to fetch Eagle.

The Ugliest Horse in the World was saddled in record time and he and Serena almost flew around the pasture, sailing over the low jumps, Serena grinning ear to ear.

So she wouldn't think I noticed, I rode Belle up to the ridge and circled back slowly, timing my arrival for the end of the half hour. When she saw me, Serena glanced at her watch, then brought Eagle over to where Belle and I stood waiting on the other side of the fence.

"You know what, Chris?" she said. "I've been thinking. Dandy is so beautiful, there isn't another horse half as pretty—except your Belle, of course. So, if I have to buy a different horse, until I ride well enough to handle Dandy, how could I find one that compares with Dandy?"

"You've got a point," I said, super casual-like.

"So I figured, instead of looking for one that's just okay, why not get one that's really kind of ugly? After all, when you're in the saddle, it's how a horse goes that really counts, not what he looks like."

"Hmmm," I said. "What are you trying to tell me?"

"I've decided to take you and your dad up on your offer, if it still stands. I'd like to sell you Dandy— just for a while—and buy Eagle from you."

"No kidding." Somehow I managed not to crack a smile. "I'll have to ask Dad if he's made other plans for Eagle though. It's been weeks since he came up with the offer."

"Oh, Chris, please! Tell him I really, *really* want to buy Eagle."

"You're totally sure?" I couldn't resist teasing her for just one more second.

"I'm positively, definitely sure!"

"Well then, Dad will probably agree. He did say he wanted Eagle to have a good owner, and he knows you'll take care of him."

"I will," Serena promised, patting Eagle's neck. "He'll have the very *best* care, because, even if he's the ugliest horse I've ever seen, right now he's perfect for me."

"You know, Serena," I said, finally letting myself bust out grinning, "I think you're right! You're absolutely right!"

LOOK FOR

The next in the
Double Diamond Dude Ranch Series:

ME, MY MARE, AND
THE MOVIE

(#5)

By Louise Ladd

Available August 2003
from Tor Books